Written by

LISA MANTCHEV

Illustrated by

TAEEUN YOO

A PAULA WISEMAN BOOK

SIMON & SCHUSTER BOOKS FOR YOUNG READERS

NEW YORK LONDON TORONTO SYDNEY NEW DELHI

For my grandmother, Harriet, the first artist I knew
—L. M.

To Boreum, with love
—T. Y.

SIMON & SCHUSTER BOOKS FOR YOUNG READERS
An imprint of Simon & Schuster Children's Publishing Division
1230 Avenue of the Americas, New York, New York 10020
Text copyright © 2015 by Lisa Mantchev
Illustrations copyright © 2015 by Taeeun Yoo
SIMON & SCHUSTER BOOKS FOR YOUNG READERS is a trademark of Simon & Schuster, Inc.
For information about special discounts for bulk purchases, please contact Simon & Schuster Special Sales
at 1-866-506-1949 or business@simonandschuster.com.
The Simon & Schuster Speakers Bureau can bring authors to your live event. For more information or to book an event,
contact the Simon & Schuster Speakers Bureau at 1-866-248-3049 or visit our website at www.simonspeakers.com.
Book design by Laurent Linn
The text for this book is set in Hank BT.
The illustrations for this book are rendered using linoleum block prints, pencil, and Photoshop.
Manufactured in China
0221 SCP
16 18 20 19 17
Library of Congress Cataloging-in-Publication Data
Mantchev, Lisa.
Strictly no elephants / Lisa Mantchev ; illustrated by Taeeun Yoo.
pages cm
"A Paula Wiseman Book."
Summary: A boy is excluded from joining his friends' pet club because of his unusual pet.
ISBN 978-1-4814-1647-4 (hardcover)
ISBN 978-1-4814-1648-1 (eBook)
[1. Elephants as pets—Fiction. 2. Pets—Fiction. 3. Toleration—Fiction.] I. Yoo, Taeeun, illustrator. II. Title.
PZ7.M31827St 2015
[E]—dc23
2013045394

The trouble with having a tiny elephant
for a pet is that you never quite fit in.

No one else has an elephant.

Every day I take my elephant for a walk.

His is a very thoughtful sort of walk.

He doesn't like the cracks in the sidewalk much.

I always go back and help him over.

That's what friends do: lift each other over the cracks.

Today I'm walking my tiny elephant
to Number 17. It's Pet Club Day
and everyone will be there.

"Come along. There's a good boy."

I coax him the last few feet. "It'll be fine."

When I look up, there's
a sign on the door.

My tiny elephant leads me back to the
sidewalk, never minding the cracks.

That's what friends do:
brave the scary things for you.

"Did you try to go to the Pet Club meeting too?"
the girl asks.
"Yes," I say. "But they don't allow elephants."

"The sign didn't mention skunks," the girl says,
"but they don't want us to play with them either."
"They don't know any better," I tell her.

"He doesn't stink," the girl adds.
"No, he doesn't," I agree. "What if
we start our own club?"

"Come along," I say, making certain that my tiny elephant follows me. Because that's what friends do: never leave anyone behind.

"We can play here," one
of our new friends says.

"All of us."

So we paint our own sign.

STRICTLY
NO STRANGERS
NO SPOILSPORTS
ALL ARE
WELCOME

My tiny elephant will give you
directions if you need them.

Because that's what friends do.